THE NAUGHTIEST UNICORN

ON THE BEACH

PIP BIRD

ILLUSTRATED BY DAVID O'CONNELL

EGMONT

Contents

CHAPTER ONE
Summer at Unicorn School

Mira Desai stared out of the classroom window. The sun was beating down from the bright blue sky, and in the distance she could hear splashes and shouting. One of the other Unicorn School classes must be having their lesson in the swimming pool! Mira wished *her* class – Class Red – could be outside. It was VERY hot, and quite hard to concentrate on the lesson. *And* they were doing a test.

A tiny bit of breeze blew through the window

and Mira smiled to herself. Even doing something a bit boring at Unicorn School was basically better than doing anything else in the real world. Because at Unicorn School everyone had a UBFF (Unicorn Best Friend Forever), and you got to hang out with them all day!

When they had been matched with their unicorns on their first day at Unicorn School (which felt like *ages* ago now), Mira hadn't been expecting a unicorn like Dave. Everyone else's unicorns had trotted out all glittery, elegant and magical, while Dave had to be dragged out on his bum. That's when Mira started to realise he was a bit different . . .

Dave was more definitely grumpy than glittery.

He *never* did what he was told and he liked to spend most of his time either eating or having a nap. He was also the Unicorn School record holder for eating the most cakes in a minute (fifteen) and doing the most farts in an hour (1,074). But Dave was Mira's UBFF – and she loved him just the way he was. Going on adventures with him was Mira's favourite thing in the world, and she always brought a bag of doughnuts to help persuade him to do things.

Currently Dave was lying on his back next to the open window with his legs stretched out, snoring and farting weakly. And Mira was finding it hard to concentrate, because as soon as the morning lessons were over, the whole school

was going on a very special trip – to the beach!
Mira couldn't wait to paddle in the sea, build
sandcastles and have loads of ice cream.

But even more exciting than that: they were going to Horseshoe Bay, which was famous for being the place where all the unicorn pirates used to hang out. They'd recently spent a whole lesson reading about all the different pirate legends and writing their own pirate stories. Mira had written about a pirate called Captain Mira Glitterbeard and her trusty First Mate Dave. In the story, Captain Glitterbeard found a giant box of buried treasure and made her annoying sister walk the plank five times.

Mira was secretly hoping that they might find some *real* buried treasure at Horseshoe Bay . . . and she knew Dave would love the beach (especially the ice cream).

But first of all, Mira had a test to finish. She looked down at her paper.

Question 10. Which animal is known as the 'Unicorn of the Sea'?

'Dave,' whispered Mira. 'Do you know the answer?'

Dave's ear twitched and he gave a little grunt.

'Dave!' Mira hissed again, but he didn't respond.

'Complete the seaside quiz in silence, please,' said their teacher, Miss Glitterhorn, from the front of the classroom. She was sitting back on her chair and fanning herself with a unicorn science textbook.

Mira stared down at the question and thought

hard. Was it a sea horse? Or maybe a swordfish?
Next to her, her best friend Darcy put her hand
up.

'Yes, Darcy?' said the teacher.

'Can we open another window?' said Darcy.

'All the windows are open, Darcy,' said Miss
Glitterhorn.

'Can we open the roof?' said Darcy.

Miss Glitterhorn ignored Darcy. Mira put her
hand up.

'Mira – what is it?' said Miss Glitterhorn.

'Is it time to go to the beach yet?' said Mira
hopefully.

'No, not quite yet,' said Miss Glitterhorn with
a sigh.

'It's so hot I can't even THINK,' said Darcy.
'I can't possibly work.' She put her head on her
desk and signalled for her unicorn, Star, to fan
her.

'I'm really thirsty,' croaked Seb.

'You have a bottle of water on your desk, Seb,'
said Miss Glitterhorn.

'Yes, but I'm thirsty for ice lollies,' said Seb.

'I'm sweating so much I can't hold my pen!' said Mira's other best friend Raheem, panicking as he tried to write and his pen slipped from his hand.

'Just whisper the answers to me and I'll write them down for both of us,' said Darcy, leaning over.

'Thanks Darcy,' whispered Raheem gratefully.

'Number 10 is *Narwhal*.'

'Ooh, I forgot about them!' whispered Mira, writing it down. 'Narwhals are so cool!'

'Their horns poke through their SKULLS,' shouted Flo, turning round from the desk in front.

There was silence, and they all looked at Flo.

'In Unicorn World, narwhals have these cool sparkly horns,' said Seb. 'Firework has a narwhal poster in his stable.' Seb's unicorn Firework whinnied happily.

'Cool!' said Mira.

'I said, work in SILENCE!' said Miss Glitterhorn.

There was silence in the classroom again until

two seconds later, when Dave let out a loud trumpeting fart and woke himself up.

'Okay, we'll finish there,' called Miss Glitterhorn from the front of the classroom, pouring herself a drink of water from the jug next to her. 'Check through all your answers.'

Mira looked back over her test paper. She hadn't been able to answer all the questions, but on the ones she didn't know she'd drawn some nice pictures of starfish and dolphins, so maybe she'd get some extra marks for that.

'Right, Class Red,' said their teacher. 'Can I have a volunteer to collect all the quizzes and bring them up to the front?'

Flo peered at Miss Glitterhorn through her

steamed-up glasses and shook her head. 'It's so hot. I won't make it that far.'

'I'm sorry, Miss Glitterhorn,' said Darcy, 'but I don't think any of us has the energy for that.'

Freya made her answer sheet into a paper aeroplane and threw it on to Miss Glitterhorn's desk, which the teacher said was 'very resourceful but not acceptable'.

'I see,' said Miss Glitterhorn, raising her eyebrows. 'Then I'm guessing you won't have the energy to come and get these ice lollies?' She held up a box of unicorn rainbow lollies. 'What a shame. I'll just have to eat them myse—'

Miss Glitterhorn was drowned out by the sound of Class Red and their unicorns

stampeding to the front of the classroom, loud

cheering, and Darcy shouting, 'I WANT

THE RED ONE!'

It was time to go to the beach!

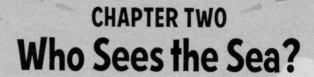

CHAPTER TWO
Who Sees the Sea?

Soon Class Red were on their unicorns and trotting through the Fearsome Forest. Mira and Dave were at the back as usual, because Dave had little legs *and* because he kept stopping to eat things. At least it was nice and cool under the shade of the trees.

Mira checked through her beach bag to make sure she had all the essentials — sun cream, swimming kit, doughnuts for Dave.

They rounded the corner that took them out of the forest and the Glitter River came into view. Mira gasped. The sun made the river twinkle with different colours, and it stretched far away into the distance. Bobbing about on the water was a boat, with a rainbow flag and a wooden unicorn at the front.

Mira felt an excited tingling in her tummy.
She would be sailing on a ship, just like Captain
Glitterbeard in her story! All the boat needed
was a skull and crossbones on the flag and a
plank and it would be the perfect pirate ship. She
wondered if the teachers would let her have a go
at steering.

Most of the other children and unicorns had
already climbed aboard and were wearing bright
orange life-jackets. Mira heard the babble of
excited chatter as she and Dave got closer to the
riverbank.

'Hurry *up*!' called an impatient voice. It was
Mira's sister, Rani. Miss Glitterhorn had asked
for special volunteers from Class Yellow to help

out on the beach trip and Rani had offered.
Since then she'd been excitedly telling Mira that
Mira had to do everything she said, 'or else'.

Mira and Dave caught up with Rani and her
unicorn, Angelica.

'Why are you so SLOW?' said Rani. Angelica
snorted impatiently.

'It's not Dave's fault he has little legs!' said
Mira as she hopped off her unicorn's back.

Rani looked at Dave, who turned around and
ran the other way down the riverbank to eat
some sparkleberries. Mira got a doughnut out of
her beach bag and waved it in the air to get Dave
to come back. Rani shook her head and sighed.

'Maybe we could sit together on the boat?'

Mira said. It didn't look like there were many spaces left.

'No thanks,' said Rani. 'I've already got a seat.'

She waved at her friend Lois, the other Class Yellow helper, and ran off with Angelica trotting behind her. Lois gave Mira a friendly wave. Lois's unicorn, Popcorn, was turquoise with a pink, glittery mane. Mira thought they were both very cool. She gave a friendly wave back and Dave gave a friendly fart.

Dave trotted back to Mira and scoffed the doughnut. Then they joined Flo and her unicorn Sparkles, who were still putting on their life-jackets.

'Can we sit with you?' said Mira.

'Oh, I think Seb has saved me a seat,' said Flo.

'Excuse me,' said a voice.

Mira and Flo turned to see a big basket standing behind them.

'What do you want, Basket?' said Flo, looking startled.

Their classmate Jake poked his head round from the back of the basket. 'Can you all get out of my way please because I'm carrying something really important?'

'What is it?' said Flo, but Jake and his giant basket carried on walking. Mira and Flo jumped out of the way.

Mira and Dave collected their life-jackets from Miss Hind, their PE teacher, who was also helping out on the trip. By the time Mira had wrestled Dave into his life-jacket and they *finally* got on to the boat, the only seat left was next to . . .

'Jake,' said Miss Glitterhorn. 'Move your basket so Mira and Dave can get in.'

'I thought maybe I could steer the boat

20

instead?' said Mira.

Miss Glitterhorn laughed. 'Very funny, Mira!' she said. 'Now sit down next to Jake and we can set sail.'

Jake rolled his eyes. His unicorn, Pegasus, snorted.

Mira sighed. Well, at least they were near the front so they would get a great view.

Jake moved his basket about two centimetres, so Dave had to sit on the floor. Unfortunately he sat on Pegasus's tail, making Pegasus scream.

Miss Glitterhorn spoke into a microphone, and her voice echoed from a speaker at the front of the boat. 'I know we're all excited,' she boomed, 'but let's keep the noise down, please! There will be Havoc Points for anyone who misbehaves.'

Jake glared at Mira. 'Make sure your unicorn doesn't get us in trouble,' he said.

'He won't!' said Mira. Jake was *always* grumbling at Dave and saying he was naughty, which was so unfair. In fact, on a couple of occasions Dave had actually got Jake *out* of trouble. Though he did also steal Pegasus's food.

Mira turned to look at her unicorn. Dave was now leaning over the side of the boat and wearing a captain's hat.

'That's mine!' said Jake, grabbing the hat and putting it on his head. He patted the basket next to him. 'I've got *loads* of cool beach stuff. I've brought all these really amazing inflatables. And they're brand new and cost a LOT of money. And me and Pegasus are going to play on them.'

'Wow,' said Mira. 'That will be fun.' She reached into her bag and found a doughnut for Dave. She was sure he'd behave on the boat, but just in case . . .

'One of the inflatables actually lets you hover *above* the sea,' said Jake.

Mira nodded. Dave balanced the doughnut on his nose, then flipped it up into the air and caught it in his mouth.

'I might let you have a go on them if you're *really* lucky,' said Jake, shrugging. 'But only for like thirty seconds or something,' he added quickly. 'And just on the sand, not in the sea.'

'Thanks Jake,' said Mira.

'And only if your unicorn promises not to break it with his giant bum. OW!' said Jake. Dave had changed his position on the floor and accidentally sat on Jake's foot.

Mira grinned and held up another doughnut. Dave shuffled over to her and nuzzled her shoe. There was a judder and a creak underneath them, and Mira looked around to see that the boat had started to move. They were finally on their way!

'Next stop, the beach!' she yelled, and the other children cheered.

∪∪∪

They'd been sailing along the Glitter River for about half an hour, and Mira was sure she could hear seagulls. They must be getting close to the beach now, she thought.

Miss Glitterhorn's voice came booming out of the speakers again. 'We are approaching the Glowing Cliffs. Among the tallest and most magical cliffs in the land, they glow in the dark to guide sailors and their unicorns home.'

As the teacher told them more about the cliffs, and they got closer to Horseshoe Bay, Mira imagined sailing her own ship on the

seven seas. She pictured the cliffs glowing in the dark night as her ship soared through the stormy waves into Horseshoe Bay. And the crew cheering as they found LOADS of glittery treasure, all thanks to Captain Glitterbeard!

Mira pictured the sand sparkling and the rockpools glinting in the moonlight. What if there was buried treasure at Horseshoe Bay? Captain Glitterbeard would be the one to find it . . .

Then something came flying through the air and hit Mira on the side of the head, snapping her out of her daydream. She looked down to see a folded-up bit of paper with her name on it. Mira recognised Darcy's handwriting. She looked to the back of the boat, where Darcy and Raheem were waving at her. Mira grinned and waved back, and then she opened the note.

Hey Mira!!!

WE MISS YOU!! We meant to save you

a seat but I thought Raheem was going to and he

thought I was going to and in the end neither of us did.

Star was VIOLENTLY SICK earlier so I've been

singing a song I invented to cheer her up! It's called I

DO LIKE TO BE BESIDE THE SEASICK.

CAN'T WAIT to hang out on the beach with

you and build an enormous SAND MONSTER!!

Raheem says he wants to also collect

rocks or something.

LOADS OF LOVE,

Darcy and Raheem

and Star and Brave

Mira grinned again and felt a buzz of excitement. She couldn't wait to hang out on the beach with her best friends and their UBFFs!

'First one to see the sea is the winner!' called Jake, standing up on his seat.

Everyone on their boat started craning their necks to try and see. Madame Shetland threatened Jake with a Havoc Point if he didn't sit down.

'What do we win?' called Darcy from the back of the boat.

'It doesn't matter,' said Jake, 'because *I'm* going to win.' He reached into his basket and pulled out a telescope.

'But what if I win?' said Darcy.

30

'You get to be Captain Jake's assistant,' said Jake.

'I'm out,' said Darcy.

'If we're your assistants, can we go on the inflatables?' said Mira.

'I saw an otter earlier,' called Flo. 'What do I get?'

'It wasn't an otter, it was a lump of wood,' said Flo's sister, Freya.

'Look, everyone stop talking,' said Jake, putting the telescope down and turning round. 'I'm Captain Jake and I always win –'

'I see the sea!' said Flo.

Mira turned to look. A glittering line of blue had appeared on the horizon. The river was

flowing right on the top of the cliff now. She could see little glimpses of sparkly sand over the cliff tops as the boat gently rocked from side to side.

Then there was a *whooshing* sound. They were all surprised to see safety barriers lowering over their seats, just like the ones you got on rides at theme parks or fairs!

'Okay, children, prepare for the final approach,' Miss Glitterhorn boomed.

'OMG it's a GIANT WATERSLIDE!' screamed Flo.

CHAPTER THREE
Horseshoe Bay

'WHEEEEEEEEEEEEEEEEEEEEE EEEEEEEEEEEEEEEEEEEE!' yelled Mira at the top of her voice as the boat tipped forward. They zoomed downwards along the rapids as the river flowed over the edge of the cliff towards the bay.

'HELLLLLLLLLLLLLLLLLLLLLLL LLLP!' yelled Raheem from the back of the boat.

The boat twisted and turned as it zoomed through the rapids. Mira's stomach did a flip.

On each side of her, the Glowing Cliffs flashed past in a blur. It felt like they were getting faster and faster, and faster and *faster*, until . . .

SPLASHHHHHHHH!

The boat landed in a lagoon just off the main beach, sending up jets of water all around them. Mira and Dave were absolutely soaked!

A few minutes later Mira climbed out of the boat and on to a wooden pier by the side of the lagoon. Dave shook the water off himself like a dog, all over Jake.

'Mind my captain's hat!' said Jake.

From the pier they could see the whole of Horseshoe Bay stretching out in front of them in a big curve. The sea was a bright turquoise blue and was lapping at the beach in gentle waves. Unicorn sand seemed extra sparkly, and Mira could see lots of glittery rockpools to explore. It was so exciting that actual unicorn pirates used to hang out here!

Above them, more and more seagulls circled, cawing loudly.

'Miss Glitterhorn,' called Flo. 'I've lost my jelly sandal.'

'How have you managed that, Flo?' said the teacher.

'I took my jelly sandals off to let my feet breathe and one just vanished,' said Flo.

'Um, well . . . you might need to hop,' said Miss Glitterhorn.

'You can borrow one of my flippers?' suggested Seb.

'Thanks Seb!' said Flo, putting on one flipper and walking lopsidedly along the pier.

They went down some steps to the beach.

'Time to get changed,' said Miss Glitterhorn, as Flo and Tamsin and their unicorns, Sparkles

and Moondance, ran down the beach and straight into the sea. 'Come back!' called Miss Glitterhorn, running after them, while Miss Hind herded everyone else towards the beach huts.

Mira was wearing rainbow shorts and a T-shirt, with a big straw sunhat.

Dave came out of his hut and trotted up to Mira. He was wearing sunglasses and a stripy all-in-one swimsuit.

'Let's go and explore, Dave!' said Mira.

But Dave had already trotted right past her and was heading back towards the pier. Mira soon realised why. There was a fish and chip shop, with an ice-cream stand next to it.

Miss Hind, the PE teacher, grabbed Dave by the scruff of the neck and brought him back.

Raheem's unicorn, Brave, was wearing a full wetsuit and flippers.

'I've got the same outfit!' said Raheem.

'You could go snorkelling!' said Mira, thinking how awesome it would be to see all the fish and sea creatures up close. Brave gave a shrill whinny.

'You don't think he's scared of the sea, do you?' said Darcy to Raheem.

At the mention of 'sea', Brave reared up and tripped over his flippers.

'Don't worry, boy,' said Raheem, patting his unicorn's neck. 'We won't go in very far. There's

nothing to be scared of.'

'LOOK, A GIANT SEA
MONSTER!' yelled Darcy.

Brave leapt into the air, whinnying in
panic. He ran behind Raheem and peered out
nervously.

'It's not a monster, it's a
pile of seaweed,' said Freya.

'Oh yeah,' said Darcy.

Brave straightened up and stood next to Raheem again, trying to look casual.

The teachers were setting up deckchairs and parasols and Miss Glitterhorn stacked up a pile of books. 'They're my beach reads,' she said. Mira peered over at the top book. The cover was of a muscly man with his shirt open, sitting on a unicorn and looking serious.

Then Miss Hind blew her whistle to call all the children over and Miss Glitterhorn told them all to reapply their sun cream while she explained the day's activities.

'Welcome to Horseshoe Bay, Class Red!' she said. 'We are going to have a splendid day on this lovely beach. First, we're going to have a little dip in the sea . . .'

'Yay!' said Flo and Tamsin, and they started running towards the sea again. This time, Miss Hind sidestepped along the sand like a crab and managed to catch them.

'Once you've finished listening to me,' continued Miss Glitterhorn, looking pointedly at Tamsin and Flo, 'we will have a little dip in the

sea. Make sure you don't go out of your depth in the water – only up to your waist, or the tops of the legs for unicorns.'

A couple of the unicorns whinnied excitedly and stomped their hooves. Brave gave a panicked snort.

'And after that, the seaside quest will begin!' said Miss Glitterhorn.

Mira's tummy did another flip. She LOVED quests.

'You will explore the different areas of Horseshoe Bay – the rockpools, the sand dunes, Dolphin Point – and there will be different types of beach activities to take part in,' said her teacher. 'Each activity is going to help you with the final, very special, part of the quest . . .'

'Ooh, is it swimming with sharks?' said Darcy.

'Is it rock collecting?' said Raheem hopefully.

Mira felt excitement rising in her chest. 'Is
it FINDING BURIED TREASURE?' she
blurted out.

'Yes!' said Miss Glitterhorn. 'The buried
treasure, I mean, not the rocks or the sharks.'

'Yaaaaaaay,' cheered Class Red. Mira jumped
up and down on the sand in delight. This was
her chance to be Captain Glitterbeard!

'And we'll also have lunch,' said Miss Hind.

Dave whinnied with joy.

Seb put up his hand. 'What is the treasure,
Miss Glitterhorn?'

'It's a mystery . . .' said Miss Glitterhorn, mysteriously. There was a hush, as they all wondered what it might be.

'Is it something rubbish like "the pride of winning"?' said Darcy.

'Can I take home this turtle if I win?' said Flo, who was stroking a large turtle.

'What? No – Flo, where did you FIND that?' said Miss Glitterhorn.

'Right – paddling,' said Miss Hind. 'Off you go. No running . . .'

She was interrupted by a loud *SPLASH* as Flo and Tamsin and their unicorns, Sparkles and Moondance – who had already sprinted all the way down to the shore again – leaped into the water.

'Ooh, Jake, can we play with your inflatables in the sea?' said Mira.

They all turned to look at Jake. He and his unicorn Pegasus were blowing up the inflatables and arranging them carefully in a line on the sand. They'd already inflated the dragon and the big purple doughnut and Jake was in the middle of blowing up a cactus with sunglasses.

Jake saw them looking. He stopped blowing up the cactus and frowned. 'I have to be really careful with them,' he said. 'I think it's better if it's just me who plays with them.'

Disappointed groans went around the group.

'Jake, it's much more fun to share,' said Miss Glitterhorn, who was back from dropping off

the turtle in the sea. 'And I'm sure that everyone would be very happy to help you blow them up?'

Jake looked up at them all, and then down at the nearest inflatable. Mira wasn't completely sure, but she thought it was a rainbow poo emoji. She reached out to start blowing it up.

'I can do it myself,' Jake said, snatching it away.

'We do have some school inflatables,' said Miss Hind, marching past them with a cardboard box.

Class Red cheered again, and then started running into the sea, despite Miss Glitterhorn shouting, 'WALK DON'T RUN!' at the top of her voice.

CHAPTER FOUR
Splashing, Swimming and Scary Inflatables

Mira and Dave speedwalked to the shore, with Raheem and Brave and Darcy and Star just ahead of them. Darcy's wheelchair had special wheels for the beach. They were bright yellow and matched her beach bag.

When they got there, Mira saw Rani and Angelica waiting by the edge of the water.

'Aren't you going in?' said Mira.

'I'm supervising,' said Rani. 'Make sure you paddle properly and don't do anything weird.'

She looked at Dave, and he jumped into the shallow water with a splash and then lay there on his back with his legs all splayed out like a starfish.

Mira saw that her sister was fiddling with something around her neck. It was the necklace that their granny had got Rani for her birthday. The necklace was a pendant with Rani's birthstone set in it.

'Mum and Dad told you not to bring that to the beach!' said Mira.

'It'll be fine!' said Rani, rolling her eyes. 'Don't annoy me or I'll give you a Bad Behaviour sticker.' She showed Mira a sheet of stickers she'd made, covered with little red angry faces.

Mira thought Rani was taking her role as helper a bit too seriously. Lois, the other Class Yellow helper, was playing tag in the sea with her unicorn, Popcorn.

There was a THUD as Miss Hind dropped the school inflatables box on the sand. A cloud of dust went up. Star had a small coughing fit.

Miss Hind went off for a run around the beach
and the children and unicorns quickly set about
taking all the inflatables out of the box and
blowing them up (well, the ones that didn't have
holes in), and then stood back to look at them.

'They're not *quite* as good as Jake's,' said Mira.

'They're awful,' said Darcy. 'What are they
even meant to be?'

'I think that one used to be a banana?' said
Raheem. 'And that one looks like the back half
of a cat.'

They went through the rest of the inflatables,
trying to work out what they were. Everyone
agreed that the worst one was the scary duck
with one giant eye that seemed to watch you

wherever you went. Even Dave was steering clear of the ones that were meant to be food, like the wonky carrot and the one that was either a chocolate bar or a long, thin poo.

'How are we getting on?' said Miss Hind, returning from her run.

'Um, they're really great,' said Mira. 'We think we might just leave them here – looking great – and admire them while we paddle?'

'Lovely,' said Miss Hind, and set off to do another lap of the beach.

Mira and her friends slowly backed away from the terrifying bunch of blow-up creatures, just as Freya's unicorn, Princess, who had been exploring a rockpool nearby, walked past and

saw them and immediately bolted into the sea.

'Paddling time!' said Darcy, zooming into the water and making it spray up all around her.

Mira ran after Darcy. Whenever she went to the seaside back home, the sea was always chilly, however sunny it was. Mira and her mum would just jump straight in and get it over with, while Rani and Dad would take about a million years, edging in a little bit at a time.

But *this* sea was perfect – it was quite warm, but still cool enough to be refreshing. The water was clear and sparkly and Mira could see little silver fish darting around her feet.

The children and unicorns ran around shrieking and splashing each other. Raheem

and Brave stayed at the very edge, just letting
the waves break over their flippers. Raheem
had brought a telescope in his emergency bum
bag, and he and Brave were taking turns to
look through it. Then Darcy found a half-
deflated beachball in the box and they all started
throwing it to each other. (Apart from Dave,
who was still floating like a starfish.)

Jake and Pegasus were still on the beach,
standing guard over their inflatables.

A while later everyone walked back up the
beach towards their towels and bags. It was time
for the special beach quest to begin, and Mira
couldn't wait!

'If you guys were pirates,' she said, 'where would you hide buried treasure?'

Raheem thought for a moment. 'In a cave, in a safe that's locked with a super-complicated computer code and protected by lasers.'

'I'd feed mine to sharks and wait for them to poo it out when my enemies had gone,' said Darcy. 'Hey, where are my sunglasses?' She looked all around on the sand. 'I left them on top of my beach bag and they're not here!'

'Maybe someone else has picked them up by mistake?' said Raheem.

'Maybe pirates stole them!' said Mira.

'I bet Jake took them,' said Darcy. 'He basically wants to *be* me.'

56

Darcy started to head towards where they'd left Jake guarding his inflatables. Then Mira realised that Jake was actually marching towards THEM. He looked red in the face and annoyed.

'You stole my sunglasses!' shouted Darcy.

'What?' said Jake in surprise. 'No, I didn't – you stole my captain's hat!'

'No, I didn't!' said Darcy.

'It kept falling off when I was blowing up my inflatables, so I put it back in the basket,

and now it's gone,' said Jake. 'So someone must have taken it.'

'Why would *I* take your hat?' said Darcy.

'Oh, I don't know,' said Jake, pretending to think. 'Maybe because you're jealous and you want to be captain and best at everything?'

Darcy narrowed her eyes. 'I don't need a hat for that,' she said.

Darcy and Jake continued to argue, and Mira and Raheem looked at each other. Who had taken Jake and Darcy's things?

But before they could say anything, everyone was distracted by a seagull pooing right on Miss Glitterhorn's head, and Miss Hind throwing a bucket of sea water over her.

CHAPTER FIVE
Beach Tidy Time

Miss Glitterhorn kept looking nervously into the sky and touching her wet hair as she handed out the grabbers and bin bags for beach cleaning, which was the first activity.

'Now, most people and unicorns are usually quite good at cleaning up after themselves and doing the recycling,' Miss Glitterhorn said. 'But sometimes they aren't, and rubbish can end up in the sea or washed up on the beach, where it is dangerous for the wildlife. And as we all know, it's important to take good care of the natural world and make sure it remains a lovely place for everyone to live in for years to come.'

Mira nodded. Back home in the normal world, she and her school friends had gone litter-picking at the beach. She couldn't believe how much plastic and bits of rubbish they'd found!

'Right!' said Miss Glitterhorn, clapping her hands. 'Off you go! Spread out to cover all the different areas of the beach.'

'I'll find the rubbish and you pick it up,' said Rani, appearing beside Mira. 'Look, there's some.' She fiddled with her necklace, and the stone twinkled in the light.

That didn't seem fair, thought Mira, as she followed her sister over to a little crop of rocks,

where she could see a few bits of litter. She was about to say they should *both* pick it up, when she noticed something strange.

'This rubbish smells delicious!' she said.

'Mira, you are SO weird,' said Rani.

'No, I mean it,' said Mira, sniffing the air. It was a lovely, salty, vinegary smell.

'I think I know what that is,' said Raheem, tapping Mira on the shoulder and pointing. There was Dave, holding a paper bag full of chips.

'When did you get those, Dave?' said Mira.

She hadn't noticed him sneak off. Mira had to admit, she was quite impressed by her UBFF's talent for getting snacks.

Dave snorted happily and offered Mira a chip. There was a loud *SQUAWK* and a flash of white. Dave gave an outraged neigh and looked up into the sky.

A seagull had
swooped down and
taken the chip!

Dave stared up
in shock at the seagull as it chomped down the
chip, gave another squawk and swooped away.
Dave shook his hoof at it. He hugged the paper
bag close to his chest and carried on stuffing the
chips into his mouth.

They managed to pick up all the litter in their
zone pretty quickly. Mira even managed to get
her sister to pick up one small piece of rubbish.
Soon they all brought their bags back over to
the recycling area, where they sorted everything
into the different bins.

Mira reached out to take Dave's chip bag and put it in the paper bin. And she saw that he now had an ice cream!

'He's going to be too full for lunch,' said Rani.

Mira and Dave looked at each other and laughed. Dave was NEVER too full for lunch. Rani gave them two Bad Behaviour stickers for disrespecting her, which Mira put straight in the recycling bin while her sister wasn't looking.

But as they laughed, there was another flash of white and a flurry of feathers.

Dave looked down at his hoof. The seagull had taken the whole scoop of ice cream, leaving Dave with just the empty cone.

'NEIGH!!!' cried Dave, falling to his knees

and waving the cone in the air.

The seagull swooped back and took the cone.

ᴗᴗᴗ

'Well done, Class Red,' said Miss Glitterhorn. 'You've picked up so much!'

As well as sorting everything into the different bins, they kept a pile for all the bits of rubbish they thought they could take home and turn into something else.

'I found this old tin, which could be recycled as a pen pot,' said Raheem.

'I'm going to wash all these old bottles to put my slime collection in,' said Seb.

'I'm going to dry out this seaweed and turn it into a wig,' said Flo.

65

'Dave spent the whole time eating and he's going to recycle it into poo,' said Mira.

'All lovely ideas,' said Miss Glitterhorn, and Miss Hind nodded. 'But I'm sure you're all wondering how this helps us with the buried treasure.'

Mira nodded and clapped her hands happily.

'Now, did anyone find anything that might be a clue?' said Miss Glitterhorn.

Class Red all looked at each other, and then at the pile of things they'd found.

Mira thought hard, trying to remember everything she knew about pirates. *Buried treasure . . . X marks the spot . . .* 'Treasure map!' she yelled. 'Maps are made of paper. I bet there's a

treasure map in the paper bin!'

'Yes! You get in the bin and I'll supervise,'
said Rani.

'Um,' said Miss Glitterhorn, but Rani was
already giving Mira a leg up. Mira climbed
into the paper and card bin. She started sifting
through, looking for anything that could be a
treasure map.

'Is it this little gold box that says "CLUE" on it?' said Flo.

Mira popped her head out of the bin and saw that Flo was holding up a glittery box.

'Yes, well done Flo!' said Miss Glitterhorn.

'Sparkles found it near the seaweed!' said Flo, grinning.

It was super exciting, but Mira wished Flo had said something before she got in the bin. She climbed out again as everyone crowded round Flo to see the box.

Flo pushed the little catch on the box and it popped open. Inside was a folded-up piece of paper. Flo unfolded it and held it up.

'I bet the dotted line leads to the treasure!' said Mira.

'What's a fort?' said Tamsin.

'It's when you do four farts in a row,' said Flo.

'And it's a castle,' said Freya.

'The dotted line starts where we're standing,' said Raheem, 'so I think if we follow it we'll find the fort and the next part of the map.'

'Well, let's get going then!' said Mira impatiently.

'We're going to break for some lunch first,' said Miss Glitterhorn. 'And reapply our sun cream.'

'Can't we have lunch after the treasure hunt?' pleaded Mira. Captain Glitterbeard wouldn't stop for lunch when there was buried treasure to find!

Dave stared at Mira. He farted in outrage and the sound echoed around the cliffs.

'There's always time for fish and chips,' said Miss Glitterhorn, and she led them back over to where they'd put their towels. All the way back, Dave was looking at Mira and shaking his head.

CHAPTER SIX
Pirate Thief...

A little while later, everyone was tucking into their fish and chips. But Miss Glitterhorn looked a bit annoyed and confused.

'I just don't understand it,' she said. 'Who would rip out the last part of my book?'

'Maybe the page fell out in a strong breeze,' barked Miss Hind.

'Maybe,' said Miss Glitterhorn, holding up the book. 'But it looks like it's been *ripped* out. And I was just getting to the good bit!'

Above them seagulls circled and cawed.

'What's Dave doing?' said Darcy, pausing with a chip in her hand.

Mira turned to look. Her UBFF was scoffing his lunch as usual, but he had something very unusual on his head. It was an old straw hat with a broken umbrella sticking out of it.

'I think he's protecting his lunch from the seagull,' said Mira. 'He must have got that stuff from the rubbish we found.'

'Good recycling, Dave,' said Raheem.

Dave snorted and carried on eating.

'It's strange that someone would take the last page of Miss Glitterhorn's book,' said Raheem. 'Who do you think it was?'

'I think it was Miss Hind,' said Darcy.

'How come?' said Mira.

'No reason,' said Darcy, shrugging.

'She was with Miss Glitterhorn when we were beach-cleaning,' said Raheem. 'It can't have been her.'

'Maybe Dave ate it?' said Darcy.

They looked over at Dave, who was managing to eat quite a lot of the paper bag along with his chips.

'I feel like if Dave was going to eat a book, he would eat the whole thing, not just one page,' said Raheem thoughtfully. The others nodded in agreement. 'And anyway, he was with us, getting robbed by the seagull.'

'You know, a few things have been going missing, haven't they?' said Mira. 'Jake's hat, Darcy's sunglasses.'

'Trevor,' said Flo, sadly.

'Who's Trevor?' said Mira.

'My jelly sandal,' said Flo. 'Still got Jim though.' She wiggled her other foot.

'And now Miss Glitterhorn's book page has gone too,' said Darcy. 'You know what this means? There's a thief on the beach!'

'Or . . . a pirate!' said Mira.

Raheem laughed. 'I think the teachers would have spotted a pirate!'

Mira thought for a moment. 'Not if they're in disguise!' she said.

There was a loud caw, and the seagull swooped down. It landed on top of Dave's broken umbrella hat. It hopped to the edge of the umbrella and then leaned over, looking at Dave upside down. It blinked its beady eyes. Dave glared and put his fish and chips behind his back.

Another seagull landed on the other side of the umbrella, leaned down and grabbed Dave's whole piece of fish in its beak. The two seagulls flew off together. Dave couldn't believe it!

Miss Glitterhorn came back over, and started handing out tokens. 'These are for ice cream,' she said. 'You have one token for yourself and one for your unicorn.'

'Let's go get our ice creams!' said Darcy.

Star gave an excited whinny, and Dave ran over to give Darcy a happy lick.

On their way, they passed Rani and Lois coming back with their ice creams. 'I got the last rainbow one!' sang Rani, waving the cone in Mira's face. Then she had to quickly move her hand back, as Dave made a lunge for the ice cream.

Mira stuck out her tongue. 'I hope the mystery pirate thief takes ALL your stuff!' she said.

Rani raised an eyebrow. 'I don't even know what you're on about.'

Mira and her friends got their ice creams at the stand. There weren't any rainbow ones left, but Mira got a glitter lolly that was really yummy.

The jolly woman working at the ice-cream stand gave Dave three massive scoops of chocolate ice cream, which only just about fitted in the cone, and loads of toffee sauce, because she thought he looked 'sweet'. Her jolly-looking unicorn gave Dave a hoof-five.

They got back to the towels and everyone was

ready to go.

'Rani and Lois are in charge,' said Miss Glitterhorn, pulling out her book, 'while Miss Hind and I are staying here to catch up on some marking.'

Miss Hind snored loudly from her sun lounger.

'Right, follow me everyone,' said Rani. 'Where are we going?'

'This way!' called Mira, holding up the bit of map and pointing.

Rani took the piece off her, and then Mira took it back, and they kept on fighting over it until Miss Hind opened one eye and yelled out that they had to share. They each held on to one side of the small scrap.

'Let's go,' said Rani.

'To the fort!' cried Class Red. Dave did four farts in a row.

Finally, they were on the trail of the treasure!

ᑌᑌᑌ

Class Red, Rani and Lois walked along the sand, following Mira and Rani's directions as they were still both holding the piece of map.

'Is everyone following?' said Rani.

'Jake stayed behind to guard his inflatables,' said Freya.

'That's so ridiculous,' said Darcy. 'Who would steal his inflatables?'

'You just tried to take one!' said Raheem.

'That's different. I thought we might need it

for the quest,' said Darcy.

Soon they reached the end of the dotted line. It had taken them closer to the shore, where they'd been paddling earlier.

'There's no fort!' said Tamsin, sounding disappointed.

There was something, though. Mira could see some colourful shapes lying on the sand ahead.

'Buckets and spades,' said Rani. 'What use is that?'

Mira thought for a moment. 'We must have to *build* the fort,' she said. 'Like a sandcastle!'

'That's exactly what I was going to say,' said

Rani. 'I'll design the castle and you all build it.'

CHAPTER SEVEN
On the Treasure Trail!

Darcy asked if they had to build castles or could it be something less boring, like a giant shark. Rani said it had to be sandcastles and gave Darcy a Bad Behaviour sticker. Then Flo said she'd like to make a herd of sand-sloths, and eventually they agreed that everyone could just make their own thing.

Mira had to admit that Rani and Lois's castle did look quite impressive. They dug a moat and managed to channel water from the sea to flow into it. Mira teamed up with Darcy, but they couldn't decide what to make and ended up with a half-mermaid, half-sea monster with the head of a kitticorn.

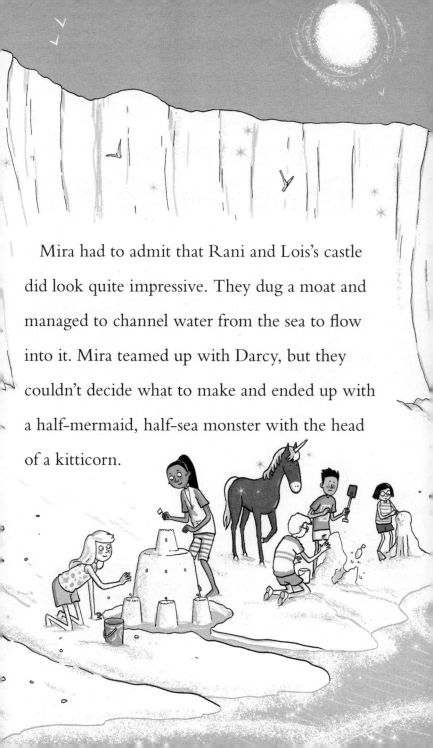

Dave just dug a massive hole and then sat in it so he could hide from the seagull and eat his ice cream. But the seagull dug a hole next to him, tunnelled through and took the ice cream anyway.

Sparkles, Flo's unicorn, found the next gold box in the sand while they were making their third sand-sloth. Inside was another piece of the map. Raheem stuck it to the first piece of map using the sticky tape he always carried in his emergency bum bag.

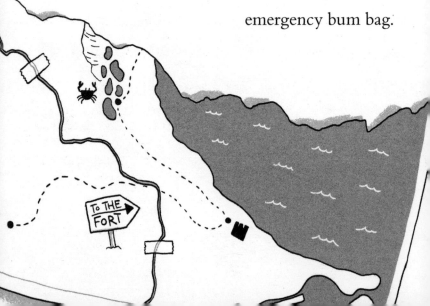

The dotted line led them away from the shore and towards the Glowing Cliffs. At the bottom of the cliffs were what looked like loads of rockpools.

'I guess we have to go rockpooling,' said Darcy, consulting the map.

Raheem nodded excitedly.

'And find a venomous sea monster,' Darcy continued, pointing at the picture on the map.

Raheem blinked. 'I'm going to look for rocks,' he said. 'They're just as interesting as sea monsters.'

Raheem and Brave went looking for interesting rocks, while Darcy and Star searched for venomous sea creatures. Mira was collecting

seashells in different colours, while Rani sat on a rock and said Mira had to bring her the prettiest

ones. (Mira gave her a few but kept her favourite ones in her pocket.)

Dave was looking for things he could eat. He tried to eat a sea cucumber and was squirted in the face. Next he tried to eat a sea urchin and got prickled, and then he ate some seaweed and disturbed a crab, which pinched him on the bottom.

'Dave, you found a hermit crab!' said Mira, coming over as her unicorn rubbed his bottom with his hoof. 'They're so cool – they find different shells to live in!'

The hermit crab scuttled out of the small, grey sea-snail shell it was in, and into a big white and orange shell that was lying empty nearby. It popped its antennae out and clicked its claws.

'It got an upgrade!' said Darcy.

Then there was a shout from a nearby rockpool. Seb's unicorn, Firework, had found the next clue box! This part mentioned 'a duel' which all the children thought sounded very exciting.

'Quick, everyone,' said Rani, grabbing the map. Mira grabbed the other side of it and

A DUEL, ME HEARTIES!

TO THE FORT

they started to run along the beach as fast as they could.

'Dave isn't here!' said Raheem.

Mira let go of the map.

Had they lost Dave? She looked all around the rockpools and squinted back along the beach to where the teachers were sitting.

'Shall we ask Basket if it has seen Dave?' said Flo.

Mira saw that she was pointing to Jake's basket, which was upside down and walking next to Flo. Mira looked down to see a pair of familiar little hooves poking out of the bottom.

She lifted the basket up.

'Dave!' she said.

Her unicorn was holding the basket over his head and eating a stick of rock.

'Like a hermit crab!' said Mira, grinning.

'So weird,' said Rani. She ran off ahead with the map.

ᑌᑌᑌ

When they caught up with the others, Miss Hind was there, looking refreshed from her nap. The last activity was beach volleyball, and Class Red were setting up the net. The weird, rubbish school inflatables were lined up on the beach like a sort of spooky crowd.

'Let's put the net in the sea!' said Seb.

Miss Hind shrugged. Darcy cheered up at this, after being disappointed that the 'duel' arrow on the map didn't mean real sword-fighting. Rani changed into her swimming stuff. She didn't want to miss out on paddling this time.

The beach volleyball game was really fun, even though Darcy kept being told to sit out. First for being 'too enthusiastic', then for being 'too competitive', and then for accidentally hitting Miss Hind in the face with the ball. Mira was pleased to hit some good shots and Raheem and Brave ventured a little way into the sea to join in. Dave had immediately gone into his starfish pose and fallen asleep, but even he won a point when the ball bounced off his tummy.

At the end of the game, they waded back out of the water and walked over to their towels. Mira was just wondering where they would find the next bit of the map, when there was a loud cry.

Mira recognised the voice.

'My necklace!' sobbed Rani.

Mira ran over. Her sister was holding up the chain of her necklace, and it took Mira a few moments to realise what was wrong.

The birthstone pendant had gone!

Rani was scrambling around on the sand. 'It was just here on my bag . . . I took it off to go in the sea.' She put her head in her hands and burst into tears.

'Don't worry,' Miss Glitterhorn was saying.

'It must have slipped off the chain. I'm sure we'll find it.'

Rani's friends were all looking through their bags and shaking out their towels. Mira and her friends started searching in the sand.

Rani sniffed and wiped her eyes. 'What if someone's taken it?' she said. 'Mum and Dad are going to be so angry. And Granny will be so sad.'

Mira felt bad for Rani (even though she HAD told her sister that she shouldn't be wearing her special pendant to the beach). What if someone *had* taken it? But before she could say anything, they were interrupted by another cry.

'We found the last bit of the map!' called

Tamsin. 'It was in the volleyball bag!'

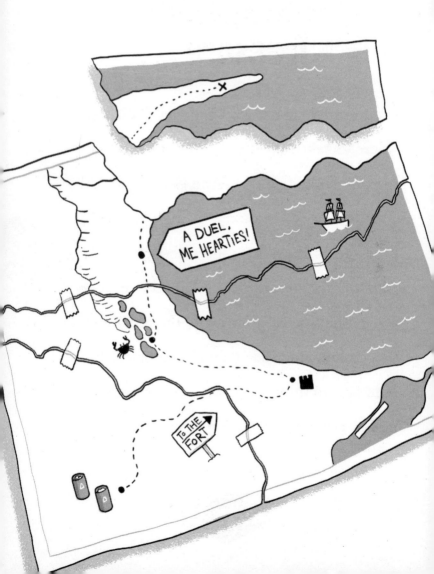

CHAPTER EIGHT
Unexpected Treasure...

'X marks the spot!' Mira turned to her sister. 'What if we find the buried treasure? How awesome would that be?'

Rani took one last look through her bag. Then she nodded and stood up, wiping her nose. 'Let's go find the treasure then,' she said with a sniff. She started marching over to where the rest of their group was. 'Come *on*!' said Rani, turning round to Mira and Dave. 'I don't want to lose because you're being slow.'

They joined the others, who were hunting around on the sand.

'The last bit of map's gone!' said Tamsin.

They couldn't find the bit of map anywhere, and decided it must have blown out of Tamsin's pocket and into the sea. There was no dotted line to guide them, but they knew they needed to go to the opposite end of the bay, where Dolphin Point was.

It was the furthest that they had walked along the beach so far, and they were near the very end of the horseshoe shape. They walked up over sand dunes, and had fun sliding down them. Then the beach rose up again and formed a spit of land that stretched out into the sea like a pier.

This was Dolphin Point.

Flo and Tamsin wanted to see if they could see some dolphins, but Rani said there wasn't time and gave them Bad Behaviour stickers.

'Oh, cool, thanks!' said Flo, proudly sticking hers on her T-shirt.

'So, the X is somewhere around here,' said Rani frowning. 'But where?'

On the other side of Dolphin Point was a big dip with more rocks poking through the sand and large pools of seawater. Just before the edge of the cliffs there were some sea caves.

'The caves would be a great place to hide treasure,' Mira said, as she imagined unicorn pirates carrying giant chests of glittery gold

coins over the rocks.

'Yes, but there weren't any sea caves on the map,' said Rani. 'We know the X is this side of Dolphin Point, so we just need to split up and look for it. Go!'

The unicorns all walked in circles around the bit of the beach where the X was supposed to be. Except for Dave. He was eating his stick of rock and holding a beach ball. Mira had no idea why he'd brought that. Dave didn't usually play sport unless he was made to.

'Come on, Dave,' she said, giving him a nudge on the bum. 'Maybe you'll find the treasure.'

But Dave wasn't listening – he was staring up at the sky. Then Mira heard the familiar cawing sound. The seagull appeared. It hovered in the air and blinked its beady eyes at Dave. Dave threw the beach ball at it and kept eating the stick of rock. The seagull turned in the air and kicked the ball right back at Dave. The ball bounced off Dave's nose and knocked him backwards. As he fell, the seagull grabbed the stick of rock and flew off with it.

ᑌ ᑌ ᑌ

'I think we've found it!' yelled Freya.

There was seaweed strewn across the sand which

was sort of in an X-shape, if you squinted at it.
Everyone gathered round, holding their breath.

'Get the spades! THE SPADES!' shouted Rani
desperately.

All the children looked at each other.

'We forgot to bring any,' said Tamsin.

'Then you have to dig with your hands!' said
Rani. 'Come on, Mira.'

Mira looked at her sister. 'Why do I have to
dig with my hands? Why can't YOU dig with
YOUR hands?'

'I'm holding the map!' said Rani. And she
picked up the map again.

Mira sighed and sank to her knees.

Dave burped loudly.

'Yes, thank you for that helpful contribution,' said Rani.

'I think Dave's trying to get our attention!' shouted Raheem.

They turned to look at Dave, who was holding something out to Mira. It was lots of chip forks all tied together with a strand of seaweed.

'You made a spade, Dave!' said Mira, feeling proud of her little unicorn.

Dave burped happily.

'How many portions of chips did he HAVE?' said Rani.

Mira took the chip-fork spade and started to dig. Then she felt the spade catch on something . . .

'There's something in here!' Mira shouted.

Everyone leaned in. Rani put the map down again and plunged her hand into the hole Mira had dug. She felt around, and then pulled her hand out again, waving something in the air. Mira peered closer again. The buried treasure was . . .

'A sock?!' said Rani.

They all stared at the sock as it flapped around in the sea breeze. It was blue, with holes in the toes and a picture of a cat on it.

'Is there something else down there?' said Darcy.

'I don't think so,' said Rani, feeling around in the hole. She sighed. 'I'll put it back.'

She dropped the sock back into the hole.

'You can't put it back. It's buried treasure!' said Flo.

'It's not. It's rubbish!' said Rani. 'We must have dug in the wrong place!'

'We need to keep the beach clean, though,' said Freya. 'Let's keep it.'

'Fine!' said Rani. She picked the sock up again. 'Who wants to carry the stupid sock?'

Mira put her hand up, as she hadn't had anything to do in the quest so far really, so at least carrying a sock would be something. Rani threw it at her.

'Right, keep looking for the X!' Rani said.

The children and unicorns started walking

around again, searching the sand for anything that looked a bit like an X. Every now and again they thought they'd spotted it, and everyone would run over, and one of them would dig. But each time it was disappointing and there was no treasure.

Mira sighed. She'd really wanted to find the buried treasure. And she wanted to find Rani's necklace, too. No matter how much her sister annoyed her (which was 100%, every single day), she knew how bad she must be feeling.

Mira's thoughts were interrupted by a strange sound. She blinked out of her daydream, confused for a moment. And then she heard it again. A low whistling sound followed by clicks.

She looked over to the rest of her group. They were halfway across the little spit of land that jutted out from the coast to form Dolphin Point. The sound couldn't have come from them.

'Did you whistle, Dave?' Mira asked.

Dave frowned and shook his head.

The whistling came again. Mira listened. It sounded like it was coming from the other side of Dolphin Point.

Mira ran up over the sand dune and looked out at the rockier part of the beach. On the other side of Dolphin Point there was a pool of seawater, and then beyond that a cave. Maybe something in the cave was making the noise?

'Come on, Dave!' she said.

She started running back towards Raheem and Darcy, who had just dug up a spoon.

'I can hear something in that cave!' Mira shouted at her friends. 'I think we should go and investigate!'

'Huh?' said Rani, turning round.

'Nothing!' said Mira quickly.

She knew that if Rani found out, she would ban them from going and make them dig up more socks (and probably give them a whole sheet of Bad Behaviour stickers). Rani shrugged and went back to supervising Flo and Tamsin's digging.

'Listen,' Mira said to her friends.

Raheem and Darcy listened. There was a low whistle followed by a series of clicks.

'It does sound like it's coming from that cave,' agreed Raheem, cupping his ears. 'We can't go there though. We're meant to be doing the treasure hunt.'

'The others are still looking for the treasure,' said Mira. 'We'll be really quick.'

She made sure her sister was still looking the other way, and then Mira, Raheem, Darcy and their unicorns slid down the other side of the sand dune. They picked their way over the rocks and the whistling sound got louder. They could hear the slow *drip drip* of water in the cave, and seagulls cawing overhead. Dave looked up into the sky and narrowed his eyes.

The sea puddles were bigger and deeper than they'd looked from up on the sand dune.

'I think the tide might be coming in . . .' said Raheem, lowering his voice so Brave wouldn't hear.

'We'll be super quick. It will be fine!' said Mira.

Dave stepped into the next puddle and completely disappeared.

Mira and Raheem fished him out. Darcy decided to ride on Star's back as her wheels kept getting stuck in the gloopy sand.

'Well, we're nearly at the other side now,' said Mira, trying not to worry about how they'd get back.

They were at the bottom of the Glowing Cliffs and the rocks sparkled and glistened in the sun. The sea was lapping at the cave entrance, and the unicorns sloshed through it.

Mira poked her head around the opening to

the cave, and gasped.

A shallow lagoon filled about half of the bottom of the cave. And in the lagoon, swimming around in circles, was a little narwhal!

'I don't think she can get out!' said Mira.

Between the pool of water and the cave entrance was a small shelf of sand. The narwhal would swim near it, poke her head up out of the water, whistle in a shrill, panicky way, and then swim away again.

'She must have got left behind when the tide went out,' said Raheem. The others turned to look at him. 'Narwhals live in these groups called pods,' he explained. 'Maybe she got separated from her pod somehow and she's trying to call them back?'

The narwhal squealed and clicked again.

'Shall we help her out of the cave so she can swim and find them?' said Darcy.

Mira crouched down at the edge of the water and held out her hand. 'Hey little narwhal,' she said, 'Don't worry – we can help you out.'

The narwhal stopped swimming and popped her little head out of the water. She blinked at Mira, and then started swimming cautiously towards her. But just as she got near the entrance to the cave, a wave crashed in, splashing all the way up the sides of the cave. They all screamed, and the unicorns whinnied. The narwhal squealed and swam away, right to the back of the cave. All the sounds echoed around, bouncing off the rocks.

Mira looked over at the narwhal again, who was cowering under the water. 'I think she

might be too scared to swim out on her own,'
she said.

The narwhal blinked at Mira again, and
nodded.

'But we can't swim out there with her,' said
Darcy.

Another wave crashed in, and the narwhal
squealed again. Again the sound echoed around
the cave.

They needed to help the little narwhal, and
fast!

CHAPTER NINE
Lost at Sea?

'Wait a minute . . .' said Mira, as the echoes subsided. She looked around the cave, and then through the entrance out to sea. 'What if we could call the pod back? The cave makes the sounds louder, so maybe if we all do it, then they'll hear?'

'That's awesome!' said Raheem.

'Great plan, Mira!' said Darcy. 'What sounds do we need to make, Raheem?'

'They communicate through whistles, squeaks, clicks and bangs,' said Raheem.

'I'll sing the theme tune from *The Little Mermaid*,' said Darcy.

'Okay, let's start!' said Mira.

The three friends started whistling, squeaking, clicking their tongues and banging on the walls of the cave. Darcy sang songs from *The Little Mermaid* and Brave and Star screeched along (unicorns love singing, but are terrible at it). Dave did his best burps. The sounds echoed loudly around the cave. It was like a music lesson gone wrong.

Mira crept back to the entrance and peered out to sea. The blue water stretched out so far in every direction, it was hard to pick out anything. But then she saw it. Very far away on

the horizon, shapes breaking through the water.
Mira squinted. She was sure they had horns.

'I think I can see the pod!' she called.

Everyone started whistling and clicking even
louder. It looked like the little shapes were getting
closer. It was so hard to tell . . . but yes, Mira was
sure now. The pod was swimming back.

'It's working!' she said.

The narwhal squealed in delight.

There was an almighty CRASH as another
wave hit the cave. Water splashed up the sides of
the rock into everyone's faces. Mira spluttered
and coughed.

'GROSS!' said Darcy, spitting out the salty
sea water.

Mira rubbed her eyes and looked out to the horizon. The pod was further in the distance now! They started up the sounds again, but it was no use. The pod was swimming away.

'We need more of us,' said Darcy. 'Let's get EVERYONE ELSE!' she said, throwing her arms wide.

Star copied her and gave a big whinny.

'There's a bit of a problem with that . . .' said Raheem, looking out of the cave entrance.

While they'd been in the cave, the tide had come in further. Now the sea puddles on the beach had formed a big lagoon.

'What do we do?' said Raheem, sounding worried.

Mira didn't know what to say. How would they get back? Had she got them all into danger?

But then she saw someone appear at the top of Dolphin Point. It was Rani, followed by Angelica.

Mira gulped. She knew her sister was the most likely person to get them into trouble with the teachers. But that didn't matter now. Captain Glitterbeard would do what she had to do to save her crew!

They all yelled and jumped up and down to get Rani's attention. Rani looked over. Even from here Mira could tell that she was confused and surprised to see them.

'Get help!' shouted Mira, waving her arms and

the sock. But Rani just waved back.

'Get the teachers!' yelled Raheem.

Darcy elbowed him. 'No, just get a MASSIVE BOAT,' she screamed.

Rani turned round and ran the other way down the sand dune, quickly followed by Angelica. Mira just had to hope that her sister would bring help. And they wouldn't get into *too* much trouble . . .

She scanned the horizon. 'The pod is getting further away,' she said. 'I hope the others get here in time!'

'We can keep on calling the pod while we wait,' said Raheem.

Back in the cave, the unicorns had climbed

into the pool to keep the narwhal company.
Dave was teaching the narwhal to float like
a starfish. He was also filling the pool with
bubbles so it was like a little jacuzzi. As soon as
Brave and Star realised where the bubbles were
coming from, they quickly climbed out.

Mira, Raheem and Darcy started up their weird orchestra again. The narwhal poked her head out the water hopefully. Mira closed her eyes and focused on whistling and clicking as loudly as she could.

'Mira!' called Raheem. 'Come and look at this!'

Mira opened her eyes. She clambered over to the cave entrance where Raheem was standing. Then she looked out around the edge of the rocks, and gasped.

Heading towards them was a line of bright, colourful shapes sailing across the shallow beach lagoon. Jake's special inflatables! There was the cactus, the donut, the dragon, the poo emoji,

and many more, with their classmates sitting
aboard and the unicorns pulling them along. At
the front of the fleet, sharing an inflatable pirate
ship, were Rani and Jake, pulled by Pegasus and
Angelica.

The inflatables made it across the lagoon. Everyone climbed off and made their way into the cave.

'Budge up!' said Rani, shuffling along the rock.

'I can't!' said Mira, who was squashed up next to Raheem.

It was a squeeze getting everyone in the cave, but they managed it. Mira and Raheem explained the problem. Then they demonstrated the sorts of sounds to make, to attract the narwhal's pod back to the cave. The little narwhal joined in.

'Okay?' said Mira, checking that everyone understood. 'Go!'

The children and unicorns started to make their sounds. The noises boomed and banged around the cave, the rocks vibrated and the air buzzed with sound. Mira poked her head out of the entrance to keep a lookout for the pod. It felt like the sound was going all around Horseshoe Bay!

Mira squinted into the distance. There was the pod, leaping out of the water. They were still so far away! But as the noise continued to echo around the bay, the little figures began to look a bit bigger. And soon, she was sure.

'They're coming back!' Mira shouted.

The whistles and clicks were joined by whoops and cheers from all the kids.

The baby narwhal swam to the front of cave, whistling frantically.

Mira saw the bubbles on the top of the water get closer and closer. Then, all in one moment, dozens of horns rose above the surface. At the front of the pod were two narwhals with very worried expressions. The baby narwhal squeaked.

'I bet they are her mum and dad,' said Mira.

The two narwhals let out sharp whistles that sounded quite cross.

'Definitely,' Raheem agreed. 'My mum and dad make noises like that when I'm late, too.'

Raheem and Mira helped the baby narwhal slide over the sand at the cave entrance. She landed with a plop in the sea and swam over to her pod. As she reached them, the narwhal's mum and dad let out a series of excited squeaks. The baby narwhal swam faster through the water. They stared at each other for a moment and then they swam together with their heads touching and their horns entwined.

★ Lost at Sea? ★

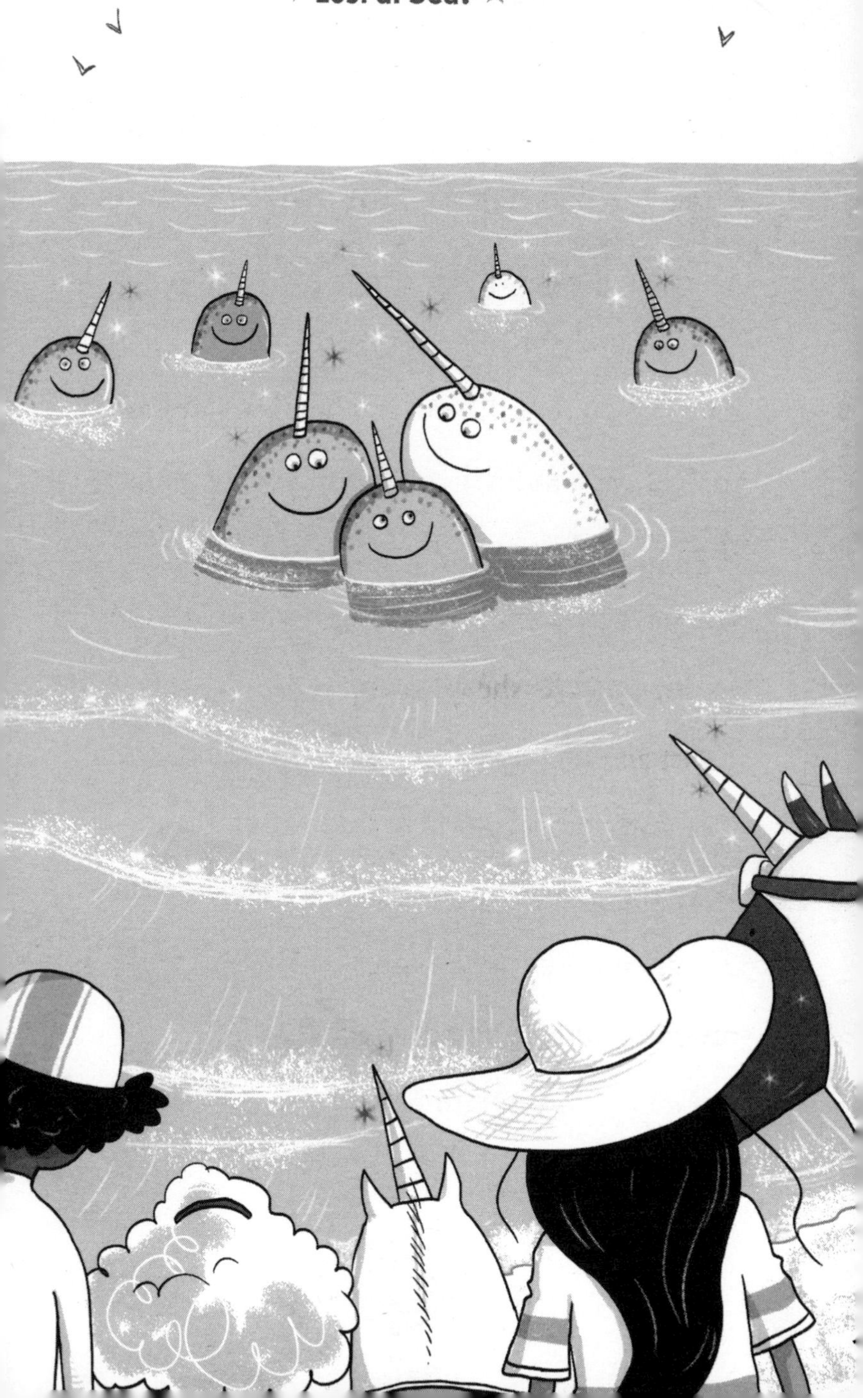

CHAPTER TEN
Happy Families

The narwhal pod all squeaked and whistled as the children rushed out of the cave to wave at them. The baby narwhal splashed around in the water, chirping and flapping her fins, and her mum and dad waved their fins too.

Finally, the narwhals raised their horns and waved them from side to side. They turned away from the cave and dived down into the water.

Mira and the others kept on waving as the pod disappeared into the distance.

'Great job, Captain Mira!' said Raheem.

∪∪∪

Moments later, the children and their unicorns all climbed down the rocks to the lagoon where the inflatables were bobbing in the water.

'We better get back quickly, before the teachers think we're lost!' said Rani, sounding a bit hysterical.

Mira thought of saying that her sister should get a Bad Behaviour sticker but, seeing as Rani had come to rescue her, she didn't.

Flo and Tamsin were climbing on to a frog inflatable while Jake checked they were sitting properly and not 'ruining' it.

Mira and Rani climbed aboard the big purple donut, and Angelica and Dave pulled them

across the lagoon. Well, Angelica pulled them along while Dave did his floating starfish pose.

'How awesome was that, Dave?' Mira said to her unicorn as they climbed off at the other end of the lagoon. But Dave was munching on a bag of crisps.

Then she heard a *caw*.

The seagull came swooping down, and snatched a crisp right out of Dave's mouth. It flew away along the rocky beach, but stayed quite close to the ground.

Dave looked at it for a second. His eyes went wide. And then he ran.

He zoomed after the seagull, his little legs a blur as they sent up clouds of sand. Dave could

move very fast when he wanted to. It was very rare that he wanted to, and it always involved food. He leaped over rocks and dodged slippery seaweed patches, heading back towards the base of the cliffs as he chased the seagull.

Mira went running after him. 'Come back, Dave!'

But there was no stopping him.

The seagull looked back, slowing down for a split second. Dave launched himself into the air, hooves outstretched. He collided with the seagull – and then the two of them tumbled over the beach, wrestling over the crisp. They came to a stop next to a rock that was covered in seagull poo and feathers.

Finally Dave managed to yank the crisp out of the seagull's beak. He jumped backwards, and then waved the crisp in the air and wiggled his bum in a victory dance.

The seagull hopped on to the rock and stared

at him. It blinked its beady eyes.

'Caw,' it said.

Mira thought it sounded sad. Then it hopped behind the rock. There was another *caw* and then the sound of cheeping.

Mira and Dave looked at each other. Then, together, they peered behind the rock.

They saw a pile of twigs and feathers and seaweed – the seagull's nest. The seagull who had hopped on Dave's umbrella hat earlier was there, too. And in the middle of the nest, there was a fluffy bundle of chicks. They were cheeping and stretching out their tiny mouths towards their parents.

But that wasn't the only thing made Mira's

eyes go wide. Poking out among the twigs were a jelly sandal, a pair of sunglasses, a captain's hat, a page from a book, the last bit of map and a sparkling gemstone!

Mira reached into the nest. The chick cheeped loudly and both the seagulls cawed again.

'Sorry,' said Mira. 'I don't want to scare the chicks. It's just that those things belong to my friends and my teacher. Do you think we could take them back?'

The seagull put its head on one side. It looked at its seagull mate.

Mira thought for a moment. 'You could have this instead?' she said, holding out the sock she'd dug up on the beach.

The chicks cheeped excitedly. The seagull reached out its beak, took the sock and dropped it into the nest. All the chicks snuggled

up to the sock and chirped happily. The second seagull cawed. Mira carefully collected up all the stolen items.

Then Dave stepped forward. He took a deep breath, held out his hoof and offered the crisp back to the seagull.

The seagull blinked. It stepped cautiously forward and took the crisp. It blinked again.

Then it wiggled its bum and started doing a victory dance.

∪∪∪

'I know it's not *the* buried treasure, but it's still pretty good,' said Mira, as they looked at the stash of stolen stuff.

'Not really, seeing as we can't keep any of it,'

said Darcy.

'You can keep your sunglasses?' said Mira.

'I'm over them. I saw some watermelon ones in the beach shop that I want,' said Darcy. She gave the sunglasses to Raheem, who put them on.

Miss Glitterhorn was a bit cross when she realised they had been into the sea without permission, but she cheered up when she realised that the missing items had been found AND that Jake had finally decided to share his inflatables.

Darcy handed Miss Glitterhorn back the last page of her book. 'Apparently she rides off into the sunset with the muscly man?' she said

'Yes, thank you, Darcy,' said Miss Glitterhorn, going red.

Jake offered Rani his captain's hat, because she had led the rescue mission across the lagoon. But Rani said he could keep it, because she couldn't really be bothered to be captain and anyway the hat had seagull poo on it. Rani was also completely distracted by her gemstone. She cried when Mira brought it back, and then spent ages turning it over in her hands, checking it was okay, and watching it sparkle in the sunlight.

'And we've got the last bit of the map again!' said Darcy.

They all climbed back over Dolphin Point. They held all four bits of the map together, and followed the dotted line. And as they reached the end of the line . . .

They found a twig.

'Is that an X?' said Tamsin.

'I think maybe it was,' said Mira. 'And the rest of the twigs are in the seagull's nest!'

Tamsin grabbed the chip-fork spade. The others came to help her, digging with their hands.

'You could have come back and got the spades,' said Miss Hind, but no one was listening. They were all too excited about the digging.

'I've found something!' said Tamsin.

She and Flo pulled a big wooden box out of the hole.

It was a treasure chest!

They popped it open, and inside was a cool-box of rainbow ice creams. Class Red, Rani and Lois and all the unicorns cheered.

Mira grinned. They had actually found buried treasure! It had been SO exciting. But then she looked out to sea where the narwhal pod had swum off over the horizon. And she looked over at Rani, who was chatting to Lois and fiddling with her necklace as they ate their ice creams. And she looked over at Jake in his pooey captain's hat as he inspected his inflatables for damage. And she thought how it felt even better helping the narwhal, and finding the things her friends had lost.

She had been a pirate, but quite a nice, helpful pirate. (Although she would still quite like to have made her sister walk the plank, just once.) Next to her, Dave finished his ice cream and did

a glorious burp that echoed around the cliffs.
Mira gave her UBFF a hug. Because Captain
Glitterbeard was nothing without her crew,
and her First Mate Dave. And maybe the best
treasure of all was getting to have awesome
adventures with your friends.

'It's almost time to go,' called Miss Glitterhorn.

Mira's heart sank. She *never* wanted to leave
the beach.

'There's just enough time for one more dip in
the sea!' Miss Glitterhorn said, smiling.

Everyone cheered again. Rani turned to Miss
Glitterhorn and very carefully handed her the
necklace to look after.

'Let's GOOOOOOO!' said Mira, and she
dragged Dave down towards the sea.

ARRR, ME HEARTIES! ARE YOU READY TO SET SAIL WITH CAPTAIN GLITTERBEARD? THEN WALK THE PLANK (I MEAN, FILL IN THE SPACES!) TO WRITE YOUR VERY OWN UNICORN PIRATE ADVENTURE!

Captain _____ and First Mate _____
        your pirate name   *your unicorn's pirate name*

went to their ship. It was called _____.
                                   your ship's name

Captain _____ met the ship's crew. There was
        your pirate name

Long Tall _____, Peg-Leg _____, and
          pirate name   *pirate name*

_____ plus _____ the parrot.
unicorn pirate name   *name*

Captain _____ pulled out the treasure map.
        your pirate name

There was an island with _____
                         describe three things you'd like to see on your island

_____. In the top corner, there was a large,

red X.

They sailed past the Glowing Cliffs, the Glittering

Headland and _____. The ship sailed through
             think up a magical place

_____! Finally, they saw the island in the
something silly

distance.

They moored the ship and jumped off on to the sand.

Captain _____ looked at the map and said,
       your pirate name

'That way to the treasure!'

The crew followed their captain through a thick swamp

of _____, battling some _____
    something silly   *describe some scary or silly animals*

_____. But the crew

bravely carried on, for this was an ADVENTURE!

Finally, they reached the X on the map. Frantically,

they dug with _____ because no one had
           describe what they dig with

remembered to bring a spade. Until – CLANG!

Captain _____ shouted, 'We did it!' and heaved
       your pirate name

the treasure chest out of the hole.

Inside the chest was _____. And Captain
                  describe your treasure

_____ , First Mate _____ and the
   your pirate name   *your unicorn's pirate name*

crew of _____ became magical unicorn
      your ship's name

pirate legends!

Catch up on all of Mira and Dave's adventures at Unicorn School!

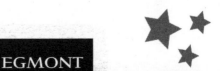

Unicorn School is getting seriously SPOOOOOOOOOKY!

THE NAUGHTIEST UNICORN AND THE SPOOKY SURPRISE

Coming soon!

PIP BIRD

ILLUSTRATED BY DAVID O'CONNELL

EGMONT
Books